M000237219

#LIFE
THOUGHTS

#LiFE
THOUGHTS

In the game of life there's winners, losers
and those who'd prefer to read this book

Avrumy Jordan

©2019 Avrumy Jordan

#LÎFETHOUGHTS

In the game of life there's winners, losers and those who'd prefer to read this book

Avrumy Jordan

©2019 Avrumy Jordan.

All rights reserved. No part of this publication may be reproduced, stored in a retrieval system or transmited in any form or by any means, electronic, mechanical, photocopying, recording or otherwise without the prior permision of the publisher or in accordance with the provisions of the Copyright, Designs and Patents Act 1988 or under the terms of any licence permitting limited copying issued by the Copyright Holder.

Published by:
Avrumy Jordan
Ozyavo, LLC
21 Ashlawn Avenue
Spring Valley, NY 10977

This book is typeset in Times New Roman and Laika.

Library of Congress Control Number: 2019911317

ISBN-13: 978-0-578-55759-5

Printed in USA

Acknowledgements

What started out with me just posting my random thoughts to a small group of friends has morphed into this, #LifeThoughts Volume 1.

I've truly been humbled that there are so many people out there that want to hear the filtered thoughts of my brain as well as getting a laugh out of them.

There are some thanks that I need to make as this book didn't come out of nowhere.

Firstly to my wife and kids. They are my greatest source of material. Thank you for laughing along with me for so long. Good job!

To my Father, you taught me so much, including the gift of laughter and being able to look at things from a different angle. I still remember the 1st joke you told me and where we were. I didn't even get it but your infectious laugh pushed me to work it out. I hope you are looking down from on high and smiling.

To my Mum, you raised me right, I went bad all on my own. Thank you. Hope I keep bringing you nachas.

To my design team. Mike, your artwork throughout added so much and brought my thoughts to life. Thank you for taking on this project.

A special acknowledgement to high school friend Mim of @40ToTheMax. It was her initial push of us turning 40 a few years ago and her encouragement to go public with my #LifeThoughts that were the impetus that got me to this point.

Thank you to the Front Page Magazine for taking the plunge and agreeing to run my #LifeThoughts every week.

To my friends, I want to thank both of you for sticking by me.

Lastly, none of this would be possible except that G-d gives me every breath.

Our Sages teach us that there is a special place in Heaven for those that make others smile. I hope that this brings you smiles. I'm counting on you getting me there. Enjoy the laughs and smile some more.

–Avrumy Jordan

CONTENTS

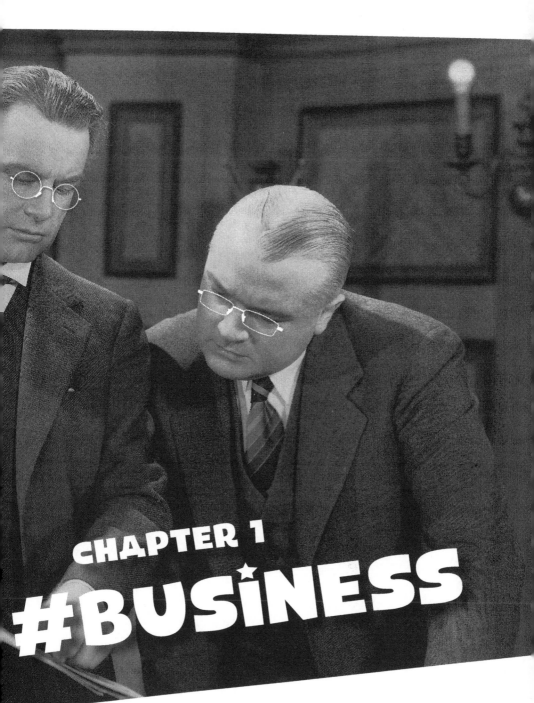

CHAPTER 1
#BUSINESS

"I have skills that I
can't put on a resume."

Sometimes I procrastinate many things at once. It's like multitasking. I call it multi-crastination and it's exhausting.

The trouble with being punctual is that there's no one there to appreciate it.

I just bought a used UPS truck... it gets poor gas mileage but I can park it anywhere

I offered to write cards for Hallmark. They said I was the reason people need cards.

Monday is a horrible way to spend 1/7 of your life.

I keep waiting for my ship to come in but all I keep getting is a canoe and one paddle.

Take care of you because if you died, your job would be posted online before your obituary.

Supervision. Not as cool as it sounds.

I paid my mortgage so don't ask me to come out with you. I'm going to sit at home and get my money's worth.

Until you have worked in retail, you truly have no idea the level of stupidity that exists in the world.

I have skills that I can't put on a resume.

Hey GEICO, why does my car insurance policy increase annually, yet the value of my car decreases?

When I grow up, I'd like to be a retired lottery winner.

Your call is important to us. Please hold for the next available agent who already hates you.

I know I'm an adult now, but I still hold out hope that money will fall out of every card I get.

I'm minding my own business. You should join me.

Business plan:

1. Hold a sign that says "free hugs"
2. Whisper during the hug, "it's $50 to let go"

So Kylie Jenner is 20 and worth $900 million. I'm 43 and just rinsed out a ziplock so I could use it again. I guess you could say we are both living the dream.

If you've ever sat in the bathroom at work and wondered how long you can stay there before someone searches for you, the answer is 47 minutes.

Money doesn't change people, it just unlocks the character that was jailed by poverty.

I think I still have some unfinished procrastinating left to do from yesterday.

Overtime? If I wanted to work I would have done it the first 8 hours I was here.

I think I'm going to add Genereal Manager of Toys R Us to my resume. It's not like there's anyone to call to prove it wrong.

Everyone claims to hate Crocs but the company is worth over $2 million. I think some of you people are lying.

Always give 100% at work but spread it out.

I'm stuck between "I need to save money" and "You only live once".

I went for an interview at Petco. They told me they were looking for a real cat person so I proceeded to slowly push all the paperwork off the desk. They offered me the job.

I text my boss every morning "Are we still on for that work thing?" His response daily is "You don't have to text me everyday. We are "on" for work everyday Monday-Friday".

A good way to make a car dealer uncomfortable is to say "Tell me if you can hear this" and then get in the trunk and start screaming.

I'm going to switch my car insurance from GEICO to Allstate then to State Farm and back to GEICO. By my calculations, they should owe me $854.

Customer service has stopped recording my calls for training purposes. They said there was really nothing to learn from that much profanity.

PSA: Don't sign anything without pretending to read it first.

People who say they'll give 110%, don't understand how percentages work.

When life gives you lemons.... take them. Free stuff is cool.

When a store says "trusted since 1982" I just wonder what shady stuff they were up to in 1981.

Who knew that rock bottom would be so crowded?

Sometimes I'll send a blank email to people to let them know I was thinking about them but have nothing to say.

How do people afford life without a job, I can barely afford one with one!

I have a friend who is very lazy. He went for a job interview and they asked him if he can start tomorrow. His response "You mean, like this tomorrow?"

The only cardio I did this week was run out of money.

It's called Party City but really it's just a store.

A panhandler asked me for $1. I checked and replied that I only have big bills. He said he'll take one of them instead. So I gave him my electricity bill! Thanks man.

Studies show that on average, humans that work in cubicles live just as long as free-range humans.

A former boss of mine once asked me if he was stupid or I was? I answered "Everyone knows that you don't hire stupid people".

Nothing says I spent the insurance money on something else quite like a garbage bag over the driver side window.

In a recent fire training meeting, when asked what to do if the building's on fire, toast marshmallows was the incorrect answer. Now looking for a new job.

Whoever doesn't believe money buys happiness, please transfer it to my account.

This florist doesn't even know anything about floors. He's acting like I'm the stupid one!

I think Target is where you pay a little extra not to be seen at Walmart.

How do people afford life without a job, I can barely afford one with one!

I may not be much help in telling you what works but I have a wealth of experience in what doesn't.

CHAPTER 2
#FAMILY

"It's like our kids can
smell us just relaxing."

Being an adult is finally understanding why Shrek just wanted to be left alone.

I wasn't born with a silver spoon in my mouth but I was raised with a wooden one on my backside.

I wish I had the time for the nervous breakdown I deserve.

I just found the toilet roll changed in my house. Now I'm concerned there's someone living here I don't know about.

I couldn't believe it when I came home and my wife told me my 12 year old wasn't mine! She said I need to pay more attention next time I do carpool.

Parenting starts getting easier when your kids are old enough to drink with you.

"It's like our kids can smell us just relaxing."

My son said to me "What rhymes with orange". I said "No it doesn't".

What is this "8 hours of sleep" thing that people always talk about?

Lazy is such an ugly word. I prefer to use "selective participation".

One of the reasons today's kids have no patience is they've never experienced the pain & frustration of trying to fold a map.

Apparently 47 empty bottles of shampoo are fine but I leave one beer can in the shower and suddenly "I have a problem".

My wife doubts my ability to repair household electric appliances. Well she's in for a shock!

When in doubt....mumble.

Everyone has that cousin that isn't your cousin but you say they are your cousin anyway.

I just learned that squirrels have 15 babies at a time. Now I totally understand why they keep running out in front of cars.

Everyone goes through life with that one thing that fulfills their sense of accomplishment. Whether it's success in a career, raising kids, being the perfect spouse, etc. Mine's having the ability to carry a zillion grocery bags from the car to the house in one trip.

If being in my pajamas by 7 pm is wrong, then I don't want to be right.

Sometimes I sit quietly and wonder why I'm not in a mental institution. Then I take a look around me and think maybe I am.

My low self esteem stems from a childhood of always being the duck and never the goose.

I think my trust issues started when my mother said "Come here, I'm not going to hit you".

At this point of my life I'm ready to believe my brother that I'm not getting a pony.

Guys, you realize you work your entire life to put a roof over your family's head just for your grandkids to call it "Grandma's house".

I finally got some time away from the kids. 2 whole hours! It would have been more but my legs were numb from hiding behind the dryer.

Don't follow my footsteps, I run into walls.

Today I had my patience tested. I'm negative in case you were wondering.

I may not be much help in telling you what works but I have years of experience in what doesn't.

CHAPTER 3
#POLITICS

"The problem with political jokes is they get elected."

Count your many blessings. If you're in Florida then recount them as well.

They still want to know what Donald Trump and Putin talked about in private. He should just tell them "Grandchildren".

The label on my bodywash said use "liberally", so I stood in the shower screaming about Russian collusion & calling everyone a racist.

With the ban on straws, what's left to grasp?

So just to clarify, if I lie to the government it's a felony but if the government lies to me it's politics?

The problem with political jokes is they get elected.

I hear ICE is switching from deporting illegal Immigrants to seniors. This will save the government millions in Medicare & Social Security besides the fact that the seniors are easier to catch & less likely to remember how to get home.

Someone just told me he wished he was David Beckham. I told him "it's 2018, just identify as him!"

Just gonna put it out there. I have a huge crush on Nikki Hhaley. If only she could become POTUS but alas that constitution thingy.

My doctor says I have a rare condition where I can read something I don't agree with and just let it be.

My most convincing arguments have been with bathroom mirrors.

CHAPTER 4
#RELIGION

"Welcome to hell...
here's your accordion."

The Chanukah miracle I'm waiting for is for us all to be able to spell it the same way.

The difference between meditation and daydreaming is drool.

If God was on facebook, I bet more people would like him than follow him.

Knowing my luck, I'm going to be reincarnated as me again next life.

For $20 I'll go to the funeral of someone you hate and start a slow clap.

So tomorrow is Monday and then it Shabbos again in 2 days?

Why do we associate Satan with heavy metal? For all we know he could like smooth jazz.

I didn't know you had the authority to judge me...Is God hiring?

If you don't pay for your exorcist, do you get repossessed?

When people tell me they are "spiritual", I usually respond "Demons are spirits too. Could you be more specific?"

In hindsight, I probably should have turned off The Book of Mormon soundtrack before giving the chasid hitchhiker a ride.

How do Amish girls know when it's a romantic candlelit dinner or just a regular one?

Religious disputes are kind of an extreme version of"my dad can beat up your dad".

On the journey through life, there are many paths to choose from. Unfortunately, many chose the psychopath.

CHAPTER 5
#MARRIAGE

"Maybe she'll laugh...
or maybe she'll kill you."

There's someone for everyone, for you it's probably a psychiatrist.

My wife is so crazy about me, she doesn't wait for a full moon to show it.

Marriage tip for you: Your wife won't start an argument with you if you are cleaning.

I was arguing with my wife & she told me I was right. What do I do now?

Do you want to know the secret to making your spouse go mmmmm all night? Duct tape!

Whenever she says "So I was thinking", be prepared to do stuff you have no interest in doing.

My wife's superpower is observing when I'm happy and putting a stop to that nonsense.

Most women are afraid of clowns...but somehow end up marrying one anyway.

My wife called and said 3 ladies at her office got flowers and they are gorgeous. I said, well that's probably why!

If I ignored you any harder, we'd be married.

My wife crashed the car today. When the police came she said the other guy involved was in his cell phone and drinking beer. The police told her that her husband is entitled to do whatever he wants while he's home.

I told my wife I want to see other people. The ER doctor said in about 3-4 weeks I should be able to again.

I bought my wife a "get better soon" card. Shes not sick, I just think she could do better.

I spend a great deal of time realizing I should have kept quiet 10 minutes ago.

My wife dropped a cup and screamed out "what's wrong with me?" Only after giving her 6 answers, did I realize that it was a rhetorical question.

I call my wife Bambi. She thinks it's because she has big brown eyes but it's really coz I want to shoot her mother.

My wife and I have been happily married for 2 years now, 1997 & 2004.

Why does my wife always wait until I'm at the other end of the house before she asks me to "merm ffrem the dfnmling"?

A man on his honeymoon was just killed by a shark. The good news is that he didn't suffer as he had only been married 2 days.

If you're wrong and shut up, you're wise. If you're right and you shut up, you're married.

Losing an argument with your spouse? Just say "my mother was right about you". That should give you the upper hand.

Before marriage: You "float his boat" After marriage: You "push his buttons"

Next time your wife gets angry, put a cape on her and say "Now you're Super Angry".

Maybe she'll laugh...or maybe she'll kill you.

Women don't want to hear what you think. Women want to hear what they think… in a deeper voice.

If you want your spouse to listen and pay attention to every word you say, talk in your sleep.

Today I gave my wife a taste of her own medicine. I took her to 10 different pubs and then went back to the first one to buy a beer.

Marriage is about understanding what irritates your spouse & using it strategically.

Marriage would be a lot easier if the opposite sex had a tail so I could see it it's wagging or not after I did or said something.

Telling her to calm down is child's play. If you want to get real, tell her she's acting like her mother.

My wife's female intuition is so highly developed that she knows I'm wrong even before I open my mouth.

When trying to difuse a bomb, I find it helps to tell her she's pretty.

A husband is sure to be right, as long as he's agreeing with his wife.

My wife asked me if her new dress made her look fat. I replied "does this shirt make me look stupid?" We are both awaiting answers.

My wife and I have been dieting together for a week so it'd probably be safer for me to come home smelling like perfume than a Snickers Bar.

My wife is mad at me…again. Guess I picked the wrong time of the month to do exactly the same things I do during the rest of the month.

My wife says I have only 2 faults. Everything I say and everything I do.

My wife got drunk last night and tried to burn our marriage certificate. She said "good luck trying to return me without a receipt".

Been having a real problem with nuisance calls recently. The most common seems to be "You said you'd be home 3 hours ago".

My wife said she needs more space so I locked her outside.

One big difference between men and women is when women say "smell this" it's usually a pleasant smell.

I find it funny how these phrases have two opposite words in them that totally contradict each other;

"Exact Estimate"

"Act Naturally"

"Small Crowd"

"Found Missing"

And my favorite..."Happily Married.

CHAPTER 6
#CHILDREN

"I don't think my inner child is ever moving out."

Whenever I'm asked to babysit, I ask if the child is a happy drunk or a mean drunk? It usually gets me out of it. Usually.

I'm still not sure why in the 5th grade at school we were taught to square dance? Anyone?

Every time my child hits a new age I think "oh look, it didn't get easier".

My best childhood memory was falling asleep on the couch and waking up in bed. I miss teleporting. It never happens anymore.

Why is it that when a child wants to show you something, they insist on shoving it into your cornea?

Some days my kids can do no wrong. Other days I understand why some animals eat their young.

So ABC recommend that you put "something important in the backseat to remind you your kids are there." Put something important there. What is more important than your kids?

My neighbor just yelled at her kids so loudly that I brushed my teeth and am heading to bed.

Babies are two extreme spectrums of smell. They either smell like heaven filled with lollipops or a microwaved porta-potty.

If you're tired & need a nap and have kids in the house, tell them to wake you in 30 minutes so they can help you clean the house. They'll do everything possible to let you sleep

Watching my kids at the park the other day and another parent asked me which were mine? Just for the fun of it I answered "I haven't decided yet". She was horrified.

Walking into my teenager's room is like going to IKEA. You pop in just to look and you end up leaving with 6 cups, 2 plates, 3 bowls and a tea towel.

I finally got 8 hours of sleep. It took me 3 days but whatever.

I don't think my inner child is ever moving out.

The only problem with teaching little kids to share is that sometimes they want some of my stuff.

If my kids knew the oven had a light, they'd leave it on too.

It costs $235,000 to raise a child these days. I'm pretty sure that's just the price of the alcohol.

I just heard a lady in Walmart scream so loudly at her kid to put something back on the shelf that I almost put mine back.

CHAPTER 7
#TRAVEL

"The point of no return sounds
like a fun vacation spot."

You know those orange cones they place on the highway for you to knock down? I set a new personal best record last night.

Wow what a relief. That knocking was coming from the trunk and not the engine.

There never seems to be a reason to "skedaddle" anymore.

Empty cop cars are like scarecrows for people.

The ability to speak several languages is an asset. The ability to keep one's mouth shut in any language is priceless.

The point of no return sounds like a fun vacation spot.

I found a hat with $17.50 in it. I thought this other guy was going to pick it up but he was too busy playing his guitar.

One day I hope to be wealthy enough not to do a double take every time I see abandoned furniture on the side of the road.

We don't talk enough about how scary it is to sneeze while you're driving.

I have my summer body now. It's the same as my winter body just sweatier.

If you're starting to look like your passport photo then it's time for a vacation.

Sometimes I wonder what happened to the people who asked me for directions.

I'm getting tired of seeing people enjoying summer. Get a job and be miserable like the rest of us.

A cop just stopped me and asked me if I knew why he pulled me over? I responded if he forgot I certainly wasn't going to remind him. Anyone have bail money?

Apparently I snore so loud it bothers everyone in the car I'm driving.

CHAPTER 8
#RELATIONSHIPS

"I just want to be wanted by someone other than the police."

This "killing them with kindness" thing is taking a lot longer than expected.

The way I see it, the more people that hate me equals the less people I have to please and the fewer holiday presents I need to buy.

I always listen to people when they're angry cause that's when the truth comes out.

The only people who ever wanted me for who I truly am are the police.

Being in a relationship is ordering a large fries even though you only wanted a small because you know your significant other is going to eat half of them even though they said they're not hungry.

One of life's problems is when someone asks "do you want to know what I think?" And you have to come up with a polite way of saying no.

Sorry...I take that back. I have no problem with the horse you rode in on.

The main function of the little toe is to make sure all the furniture in the home is in the right place.

My son asked me if a punch bowl is a place you keep names of people you want to punch. I usually keep them in my head but perhaps a decorative piece is a better idea?

You know how you can tap a YouTube video to see how long it has left? I wish that worked with people as well when they talk to you.

Gaining weight while you owe me money is total disrespect.

My therapist put half a glass of water in front of me and asked me if I was an optimist or a pessimist? I drank the water and answered "I'm a problem solver!"

Why do people with bad breath always want to whisper secrets?

I just want to be wanted by someone other than the police.

Not everyone likes me, but not everyone matters.

People who say "I hate to bother you" need to learn to hate it a little bit more.

To shake things up when you're commenting, add random quotation marks.
"Congratulations" on your baby.
Congratulations on "your" baby.
Congratulations on your "baby".

One man's trash is another man's court ordered community service.

You don't really know someone until you've said "No" to them.

I'm about to unfriend all my friends who can't reed, right or spale.

I suffer from that disorder where I speak the truth and it upsets people.

Whenever someone seems overly happy to see me, I get suspicious.

When a person with a mullet tells me they "don't care", I 100% believe them.

Instead of a sign saying "Do not disturb", I need one that says "Already disturbed, proceed with caution".

If you like to be left alone.. Just carry a doll with you everywhere you go.

When a woman says "when you get a chance..." what she really means is "get up now and do it if you know what's good for you."

Some people crave attention... and I'm over here trying to avoid eye contact.

Am I the only one running out of of people I like?

People with multiple personalities should donate one of them to people without one.

I'm pretty sure that's how all interventions start.

Hitting the gym to relieve stress isn't as effective as hitting the person that caused it in the first place.

I put the fun in funeral, the laughter in slaughter & the hot in psychotic.

If you have a parrot and don't teach it to say "Help, they've turned me into a parrot", then you're just wasting your time.

Apparently "spite" is not an answer to "what motivates you?"

Sarcasm is the ability to insult idiots without them realizing.

It doesn't matter what people call you. It matters what you answer to.

Good romance starts with friendship. Bad romance starts with "ra ra ah ah ah, ro ma ro ma ma, ga ga ooh la la".

Talking to some people is like folding a fitted sheet.

I was walking last night & took a shortcut through the cemetery. 3 girls walked up to me & said they were scared to walk so I agreed to let them walk with me. I said "I understand. I used to get freaked out too when I was alive." Never seen anyone run so fast.

Whenever someone seems overly happy to see me, I get suspicious.

One of my biggest faults is when I ask people what their name is I forget to listen to what their name is.

Revenge is beneath me. Accidents however may happen.

To make a long story short, just stop.

Pessimist: Things just can't get any worse! Optimist: Nah, of course they can!

Fool me once, shame on you. Fool me twice, shame on me. Fool me a third time, man you are good.

Duct tape: $2
Rope: : $3
Garbage bags: $3.50
The look on the cashiers face... Priceless.

I wish you could order karma like you can flowers and have it delivered.

What makes you think I don't like you? I don't, I'm just wondering what gave it away?

Just remember, they have to talk about you because when they talk about themselves, nobody listens.

Sorry I was late. I got here as soon as I wanted to.

Stop crying about your problems on the internet. Bottle them up and cover them with dark humor and sarcasm like the rest of us.

If you really can't stand someone, lend them $100. Chances are you'll never hear from them again.

They say money doesn't buy happiness but I'm accepting donations to test this theory.

I finally discovered what wrong with some people's brain. On the left side there is nothing right and on the right side, there is nothing left.

I stopped explaining myself when I realized people only understand from their level of perception.

When my friends told me I had to stop impersonating a flamingo I had to put my foot down.

I was at the dentist and he told me to open up. I responded "sometimes I get sad". I'm now looking for a new dentist apparently.

Your energy introduces you even before you speak.

I have the body of a 20 year old. Can any of you help me get it out of my trunk?

I've never killed anyone with kindness but I have knocked a Walmart greeter unconscious with an aggressive chest bump.

To the guy that stole my antidepressants, I hope you're happy now.

CHAPTER 9
#TECHNOLOGY

"I hope popcorn appreciates what the microwave did for it's career."

Why do eggs come in flimsy styrofoam packages and battery packs need a chainsaw to open?

If I'm ever on life support, unplug me and plug me back in and see if that works.

I hope popcorn appreciates what the microwave did for it's career.

With the rise of self-driving cars, there will eventually be a country song about how your car left you too.

I was today years old when I found out if you hold the 0 (zero) down on the keyboard you get ° (degrees).

I think Fitbit is just an updated Tamagotchi and the animal you are trying to keep alive is you!

No one answers their phones anymore. If I ever get arrested, I don't want a phone call, I want a social media posting.

Every selfie you post should come stamped with a number like a limited edition print. "Attempt 7 of 25"

I celebrate 4/20 on 1/5 because I know how to reduce fractions.

I've stopped explaining #Facebook to my mother. Now I say "I collect tiny imaginary people in my phone using jokes as bait"

I wonder what kids today are going to tell their kids. "Yeah. It was rough back then. I didn't get a smartphone 'til 4th grade and sometimes the wifi didn't work upstairs."

I put my food in the microwave and pressed the "pizza" button. When I opened the door it was still beans! I'm not sure what I'm doing wrong?

Is it really necessary for the f irst square of toilet paper to be glued down?

If you ever think you are useless, think of the person who writes the terms and conditions.

If we all just stuck to cursive and stick-shift cars, we could cripple the next generation.

Just as phones have "Airplane Mode" they should also have "Drunk Mode". It would make sure all your drunk texts never leave your phone. What say you

If you ever get cold, just stand in a corner for a little while. They're usually around 90 degrees.

Maybe dryer lint is the cremated remains of your missing socks?

Answering the phone "Sheriff's department, fraud division, how can I help you?" Has really slowed down the telemarketing phone calls.

By the time I find my flashlight app, I've already fallen down the stairs.

To the FBI agent assigned to watch me through my phone... either I am so so sorry or you are sooo welcome, depending on what you're into.

Every time I see someone spell a word wrong, I look down at the keyboard to see how close the letter is to the letter that's supposed to be, to see if it's socially acceptable to misspell said word.

Forget my phone, I need to recharge myself.

As I walk through the valley of t he shadow of death, I remind myself that you can't always trust Google Maps.

Scientists say marijuana lowers your body temperature. In other words, smoking weed does make you cool. It's science people.

Imagine how cocky that plastic bag that gets to hold all the other plastic bags must feel.

We can put a man on the moon yet we can't make public toilet stalls without the peekaboo gap!?

Seriously speaking though. If the world was flat, cats probably would have pushed everything off it by now.

Low phone battery warning is probably the only warning I take seriously.

Plot twist: I just emailed the Nigerian prince asking for money.

Superman could have been a doctor and used his X-ray vision to detect tumors and help people. But no, we needed another journalist?

I got so many privacy policy update emails today. I feel if I was stranded on a deserted island and a bottle with a note washed up, the note would say "we have updated our privacy policy"

My doctor just diagnosed me with low blood pressure. To fix it he prescribed 2 sets of IKEA self assembly dressers.

Why do people slap the remote when it's not working? Why does it even work after you slap it?

When a short person waves at you, is it called a microwave?

Searching for a computer online is basically forcing your current computer to dig it's own grave.

Apparently being an adult means googling phone numbers that call you rather than answering them.

When a person looks over my shoulder when I'm on the computer, I open up a new browser tab and Google "How to kill the person behind me"Remember the time when telling someone to "go play in traffic" was an insult? Now it's an invitation to film yourself dancing next to a moving car like a moron.

If you are arguing loudly in public, please put it on speakerphone. It's only fair I hear both sides of the fight.

I stopped understanding math when the alphabet decided to get involved.

The worst part of online shopping is having to get up to get your credit card.

Apparently being a adult means googling phone numbers that call you rather than answering them.

CHAPTER 10
#FASHION

"I would call my fashion
style 'clothes that still fit'."

This new fashion of guys wearing skinny pants makes me think they misunderstood the phrase "getting into her pants".

I met someone today with Summer Teeth. Summer here, summer missing.

If you're going to walk a mile in my shoes, please bring my fitbit with you. TIA.

Life lesson for you: A shot of vodka before trying on swimwear softens the blow. Trust me on this one.

Amazing. You hang something in your closet for a while and it shrinks three sizes.

I would call my fashion style "clothes that still fit".

I always wanted to lay naked on a bearskin rug in front of a fireplace. Evidently Costco has a rule against doing that.

Sunglasses are great. They allow you to stare at people without getting caught. It's like Facebook in real life.

I admire women with the restraint to draw on their eyebrows. I wouldn't be able to stop until I'd added glasses and a mustache.

I'm so poor that I rub cologne from magazines on my shirt. When people tell me I smell good and ask what I'm wearing I tell them "Page 22".

I told my wife she drew her eyebrows on too high. She looked surprised.

CHAPTER 11
#FOOD & W(H)iNE

"I'd like to see a snake eat spaghetti."

Hey Food Network I'm afraid my muffin top has become a bundt cake.

Bone in chicken wings are really just chicken on the cob.

I'm giving up alcohol for a month. Wait. Sorry. That came out wrong. I'm giving up. Alcohol for a month!

Everything I touch turns to gold. Damn these Cheetos.

If we start calling it "potato juice", then #vodka becomes a health drink.

Nutrition labels should have a "If you eat the whole thing" section.

I just heard Starbucks is going to start selling wine and beer. Apparently it's getting too difficult to sell sober people a $12 cup of coffee.

Every box of raisins is a tragic case of grapes that could have have been wine.

The Platypus the only animal that lays eggs and gives milk... The only animal that can make its own custard.

I always wondered...How many kids are in a kids meal?

Nothing says "I believe in you" more than a waiter giving you a single napkin.

People who help you find what you're looking for in a liquor store should be called Spirit Guides.

Wanted: Someone to hand feed me Doritos so my fingers don't get orange. No weirdos.

I'd like to see a snake eat spaghetti.

Wouldn't it be ironic if Popeyes Chicken was fried in Olive oil?

My backup plan is my original plan...just with more alcohol.

The difference between a beer and your opinion is that I asked for a beer.

The world is my oyster. Expensive and gross.

Cupcakes are for people who don't have the dedication and stamina to eat a whole cake!

I've just finished my research into the effects alcohol has on physical movement. The results were staggering.

My horses name is Mayo. Mayo neighs.

Never depend on people to make you happy. That's what alcohol is for.

I'm going to open an ice cream store and have flavors called "He's not worth it", "Don't be sad" & "You can do better"

I always found it super convenient that my arms came with cup holders.

Did you ever stop and think that maybe coffee is addicted to me?

I really don't see the problem with genetically modified food, I just had a nice leg of salmon.

I establish dominance at the store by never breaking eye contact with the person behind me when placing down the grocery divider.

Not to get technical but according to chemistry, alcohol is a solution.

Fun fact: Alcohol increases the size of the "send" button by 89%.

I came home to find the eggs on top of the bread at the bottom of the bag again. I've got to stop using the self checkout.

Started to go to the gym this morning but couldn't find my membership card. A new card costs $10. A coffee and donut are $3. Guess who saved $7 today?!

I hope that when I inevitably choke to death on a gummy bear, people just say I was killed by a bear and leave it at that.

Hakuna ma'vodka. It's just me and no memories for the rest of the night.

I don't know why everyone says you can save money bringing lunch to work. It's 10am, I already at the lunch I brought and now I'm going to have to by another lunch for lunch.

If you tear the box open the right way & leave it on the ground the dog will get blamed for eating all the cookies.

I hope these mosquitoes are enjoying my blood alcohol level as much as I am.

"Why isn't it working?" I whisper to myself as I start on my 3rd piece of death by chocolate cake...

When you eat a lot of spicy foods, you lose your taste. I ate at a Thai restaurant last night and later found myself listening to Justin Bieber.

When you compare the size of a gummy worm versus a gummy bear, it paints a horrific vision of the gummy universe.

I need an end of year conference with my kids teachers where we just sit back and do shots celebrating that we both survived & retained a shred of our sanity.

How old were you when you realized Arbys is just pronounced RB's, which is short for roast beef?! I was today years old.

In the event of a hurricane, put some hotdogs in your pockets, this way the search dogs will find you first.

The man that invented Fairy Bread passed away. Hundreds and thousands are expected at his funeral.

Growing your own tomatoes is the best way to devote 3 months of your life to saving $2.13.

Sometimes I turn the lights off in the kitchen and lay on the floor and pretend I'm a crumb.

A local Burger King is "accepting applications for entry level management," which I guess would be like a Burger Duke or Lord.

I don't always walk the walk or even talk the talk but if you need someone to drink the drink, I'm totally your guy and there for you.

Alcohol isn't the answer.. Unless the question is why did my neighbor run over my mailbox and park in the front yard last night.

My grandfather told me "when I was your age I worked 3 times as hard". I responded "In your day Coca Cola had cocaine in it! Of course you did!"

CHAPTER 12
#TV, MOVIES & MEDIA

"I would probably watch golf on tv
if landmines were involved."

Anyone else find it off that on Star Trek when they "boldly go where no one has gone before", they always ended up meeting someone?

I don't sing in the car...I perform.

My summer body wasn't ready.. but my fall sweater body is on point.

I always thought the expression "Dumb as a post" was about fences until I joined facebook

Does appearing on several episodes of Cops make you a reality TV star?

If California is banning plastic, shouldn't they start with the celebrities?

If you were 8 years old when "Red Red Wine" came out then UB40 now.

When Thor throws his hammer he's "serving justice". When I throw my hammer I have "anger management issues" apparently.

I just heard that M*A*S*H is owned by Fox and that Disney bought out Fox. Does that mean that Max Klinger is now a Disney Princess?

Our "forefathers" sounds like an episode of The MAURY Show.

If you work as a security guard at a Samsung store, does that make you guardian of the galaxy?

I'm so disappointed. Soulja Boy isn't a soldier, Dr. Dre isn't a doctor and I just found out Adele isn't even a computer.

I don't know how people get eaten by sharks....I mean don't they hear the music?

Honestly, my biggest fear about becoming a zombie is all the walking.

"People should just mind their own business", is probably the funniest thing I've ever read on Facebook.

Nigeria would like to apologize for their horrible results at the FIFA World Cup. To make it up to their fans they are offering a full refund of their tickets. Please send your bank account, social security and mothers maiden name to prince@nigeria.com

We all know Albert Einstein was a genius...but his brother Frank was an absolute monster.

The only good time to yell out "I have diarrhea" is when you're playing scrabble because it's worth a lot of points.

I would probably watch golf on tv if landmines were involved.

Now that straws have been banned in California, how is Hollywood going to snort cocaine?

If you play Justin Bieber songs backwards you will hear messages from the Devil. Even worse, if you play them forward you will hear Justin Bieber.

Would it be bad taste to ask MC Hammer if we can touch it now?

I learned from Tetris that when you fit in, you disappear.

People who decide to get rid of stuffed animals and leave them on the curb like garbage, have you not seen Toy Story?

'Mono' means one; 'Poly' means many; 'Monopoly' means a waste of six hours.

I think Elvis Presley shooting at his television makes perfect sense to me now.

Of all the bands named after handicapped jungle animals, Def Leppard is my favorite.

Just a reminder that if you are going Black Friday shopping, please turn your cellphone to portrait mode before videoing any fights. Thank you.

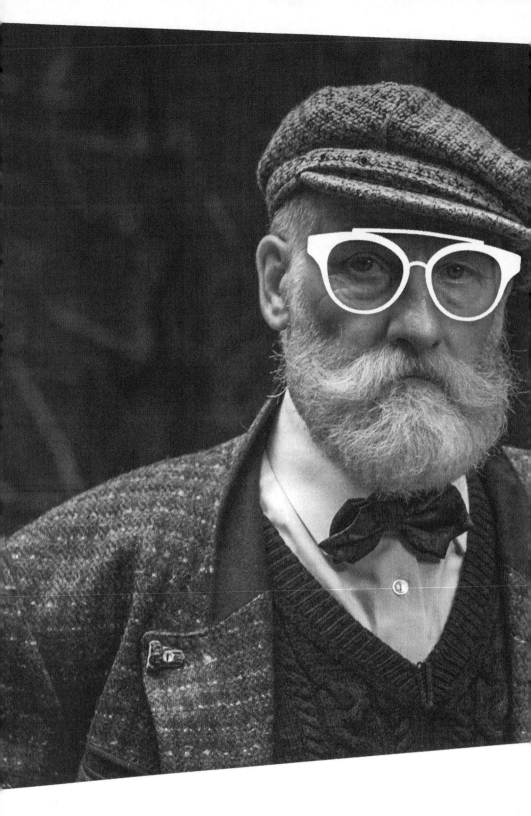

CHAPTER 13
#GETTING OLDER

"Life is just a series of obstacles preventing you from taking a nap."

They say it costs nothing to be kind. Sometimes I think it costs me my sanity.

I'm not saying I'm getting old but my family is now wearing name tags around the house.

You know you're old when you're entering your date of birth on a smartphone and you have to spin the dial like you're playing Wheel of Fortune

I try to avoid things that make me fat...like scales, mirrors and photographs.

I think the smarter you are the dumber you sound to stupid people.

My doctor told me it's not water that I'm retaining but rather it's food.

Don't bother paying a therapist. I'm happy to tell you what's wrong with you for free.

My mind is like someone emptied the kitchen junk drawer onto the trampoline.

I'm taking care of my procrastination issues. Just you wait and see.

I have trust issues because people have lying issues.

Statistically bearded men will cheat on their partner more often than bearded women.

My age is very inappropriate for my behavior.

I'm doing crunches twice a day now. In the morning it's Captain and at night it's Nestle.

Funny thing about getting older, your eyesight may weaken but yet you can see through people so much better.

You know you're old when you go shopping and see that you spent more at the pharmacy than on groceries.

I am "had to write sentences as punishment in school" years old.

I got carded at the liquor store. While getting my ID out my Blockbuster card fell out. He laughed and said "Never mind".

Getting older is just one body part after another saying "ha ha, you thought that was bad...watch this!"

Now I understand why Peter Pan didn't want to grow up.

It was a rough week. I got tonsillitis, followed by appendicitis & pneumonia. After that I got erysipelas with haemochromatosis. Then I finally ended up with neuritis Man, I tell ya, I thought I'd never pull through that spelling test!

I don't feel like I'm getting older, it's more like my warranty has expired and my parts are wearing out.

This cashier just held my five dollar bill up to the light in case you're wondering how I do with first impressions.

Some people's birth certificate should be an apology letter.

Does it count as saving someone's life if you refrain from killing them?

Some people wake up feeling like a million bucks. I wake up like "insufficient funds".

Bean bag chairs are like venus fly traps for anyone over 45.

I thought I was in a bad mood but it's been a few years so I guess it's who I am.

I believe in you. I also spent 8 years believing in the tooth fairy so don't get too excited.

I'm stuck between actions speak louder that words and silence is golden.

I've never run with scissors. Those last 2 words were unnecessary.

Starting your day with an early morning run is a great way to know that your day really couldn't get any worse.

I was at the bank and an old lady asked me to check her balance. So I pushed her. It wasn't very good.

Exercising would be much more rewarding if calories screamed when you burned them.

I'm not saying I'm old. I'm just saying that Advil is now my Skittles.

Mornings would be much better if they happened later in the day.

Whoever has my voodoo doll, please take some stuffing out of the stomach. Thank you.

If all is not lost, where is it?

I don't expect everything handed to me.. You can just set it down wherever you'd like.

If being in my pajamas by 7pm is wrong, then I don't want to be right.

I used to sneak out of bed to go to parties. Now, I sneak out of parties to go to bed.

Do you ever want to lose weight but weight just doesn't want to lose you?

Venting is what prevents me from getting free rides in the back of police cars.

I'm not broken, but I am pretty dented.

How soon after getting up is it ok to take a nap?

A Will is a dead give away.

I wish I could donate body fat to those in need.

Just spent like 5 hours introducing myself to an owl.

As you get older, funerals double as reunions.

You're only young once. After that you have to think of another excuse.

Denial, anger, bargaining, depression & acceptance. The 5 stages of waking up.

Welcome to your 50's. You now have one "good" knee and one "bad" knee.

Hot singles in your area want to run through your sprinkler.

Warning: Stop feeding your kids Rice Krispies as they don't get absorbed properly rather they are stored in your body and come out later in life. Every morning now when I wake up, my body snap, crackles and pops.

I'm in a really dark place right now. Sorry, false alarm. I was putting on a shirt and my head got stuck in the arm hole.

Your mind needs as much exercise as your body. That's why I think about jogging everyday.

I do all my own stunts, but never intentionally.

Wished upon a star to be young again. Woke up with acne on my face.

We all have abs. It's just that mine prefer to remain anonymous.

It doesn't matter if I sleep 2 hours or 2 days, I'm still tired the next day.

If you can't handle me at my worst then don't bother, because that's pretty much the level I operate at.

I know 5 people who are clinically insane....I'm 2 of them!

If I ever say "we should rob a bank" and you respond "why" instead of "how" then I'm ending our friendship.

Life is just a series of obstacles preventing you from taking a nap.

I call it taking care of myself and chasing my dreams...others call it a nap.

I came, I saw, I forgot what I was doing, I retraced my steps, got lost on the way back, now I have no idea what's going on.

"No pain no gain" I whisper to myself as I wedge my arm under the couch to retrieve an M&M.

My entire life is a pre-existing condition.

"Alcohol may intensify the effects of this medication". I never know if this is a warning or a serving suggestion.

I went to the doctor and he told me "Don't eat anything fatty" I said like "burgers & pastrami?" He said "No fatty! Don't eat anything".

Growing older is mostly just learning more and more accurate answers to the question "what's the worst that could happen?"

Interestingly, I usually blame Ambien for not doing stuff.

I believe everyone comes into our life for a reason. I also believe the reason for some of these people are to test our homicidal tendencies.

Only 7 hours 55 minutes and 35 years until I can retire.

Sometimes I lie awake at night and ask "where have I gone wrong?" Then a voice says to me "This is gonna take more than one night".

The only thing about me getting thin at the moment is my patience.

Well I hear someone screaming for help so I'm off to get more duct tape. Be back soon.

I live somewhere between "playing my cards right" and "not playing with a full deck".

You know that thing in your mind that tells you when something is a bad idea? Where do I get myself one?

The older I get the earlier it gets late.

My mind is exceptionally quiet. I'm suspicious that I'm up to something I don't even want myself to know about.

Maturity comes with age. Grey hair and back pain will give you that concerned look.

I'm not on the crazy train.. trains go fast...It's more like a wagon.. a long, slow ride on the crazy wagon.

People ask what you do for a living so they can work out what level of respect to give you.

CHAPTER 14
#AFTERTHOUGHTS

"I feel like I'm parked diagonally in a parallel universe."

I just saw a cow with a twitch. I guess it should be called beef jerky.

Why are they called leaves? They do nothing their whole life except stick around!

Sometimes I take baths because it's hard to drink wine in the shower.

My mind isn't twisted. It's just strategically bent in certain places.

I need to find more hobbies that don't include my credit card.

I'm still fascinated by the English language. Tomb is pronounced toom, womb is pronounced woom, why isn't bomb pronounced boom?

I like to confuse my doctor by putting on the rubber gloves at the same time that he does.

So after winning the game I decided to throw the ball into the crowd like I saw on tv. Apparently this is unacceptable in bowling.

Why is Sean pronounced "Shawn" but Dean is not pronounced "Dawn"?

The dead aren't scary. It's the live ones you gotta be worried about.

I feel like I'm parked diagonally in a parallel universe.

I can't do it anymore! Someone else is going to have to help prevent forest fires.

When in doubt, just do the opposite of whatever the person wearing pajamas in public is doing.

That's enough todaying for today. I've done enough.

Building a treehouse is probably the biggest insult you can give a tree. "Here, I killed your friend, now hold him!"

If it hurts you more than it hurts them, you're probably holding the taser the wrong way.

Saying "Have a nice day" sounds friendly. Saying "Enjoy the next 24 hours" sounds threatening.

I love the Halloween season, when you can dig graves in your front lawn and people just think it's cool decorations.

Apparently when you donate blood, it has to be yours.

You have to appreciate the real ones because there aren't that many left around.

Remember when you first started driving and everything was scary? Now you're going 80mph, putting salsa on your taco and driving with your knees.

Its pollen season again. You know what that is? It's the time when flowers can't keep it in their plants.

3 out of 4 voices in my head want me to go to sleep. The 4th wants to know if penguins have knees.

If you have nothing important to say, this is the best place to say it.

I bet the first guy to say "smooth as a baby's bottom" wasn't the most respected man in the community.

A sunset is life's way of saying "Good job, you survived today, here's something pretty.

If I die tomorrow, treat me like you did today.

Don't lie. You'd touch lots of freaky things with a 10 foot pole.

Sarcasm is the ability to insult idiots without them realizing.

A PSA: When being arrested and placed in the police car, don't call "shotgun". They don't find it amusing.

Omg I'm so lovable that my doctor just gave me a special jacket that I can hug myself.

I feel like there's less people putting their phone numbers on bathroom stalls offering a good time and that is why these times are so bad.

My weight loss goals are to be able to clip my toenails and be able to breathe at the same time.

I've heard it's hard being a hostage. I bet I could do it with both hands tied behind my back.

One of the Russian acrobats in our human pyramid was just deported. Now we don't have Oleg to stand on.

The only thing that keeps me from being a genius is all the stupid things I do.

If you're thinking what I'm thinking then you should probably get professional help.

Smelling is just breathing normally but thinking about it more.

I'm 500% done with today and about 68% done with tomorrow already.

Somedays I feel like a duck... above the surface, composed and unruffled...below the surface, paddling like crazy.

It's reached the point where you can no longer enjoy the simple things in life - like taking a long, slow swig of cold beer without some idiot behind you honking his horn.

Revenge sounds so mean. I prefer to call it "returning the favor".

Was the pole vault accidentally discovered by a clumsy javelin thrower?

Did you know, if your parachute doesn't open, you have the rest of your life to fix it.

I think we need to start thinking about the kind of world we are going to leave to Betty White & Willie Nelson

For the third night in a row, someone has been adding soil to my garden...the plot thickens.

I wonder what normal people think about?

Made in the USA
Middletown, DE
09 December 2019

80307561R00057